The Pet Store Sprite

PixieTricks

Read All the Magical Adventures!

Pixie Tricks

The Pet Store Sprite

Written by
Tracey West

Illustrated by
Xavier Bonet

BRANCHES

SCHOLASTIC INC.

For my nieces Lauren and Julia, who were little pixies when this book first came out. —TW

For my children, Daniel and Marti. You're pure magic. —XB

Text copyright © 2000, 2021 by Tracey West
Illustrations copyright © 2021 by Xavier Bonet

Library of Congress Cataloging-in-Publication Data
Names: West, Tracey, 1965–author. | Bonet, Xavier, illustrator.
Title: The pet store sprite/written by Tracey West ; illustrated by Xavier Bonet. Description: [New edition, with new illustrations] | New York: Branches/Scholastic Inc., 2021. | Series: Pixie tricks; 3 | Originally published: New York: Scholastic Inc., ©2000. | Summary: Violet, her cousin Leon, and the Pixie Tricker Sprite have a serious problem: The fairy they are dealing with now is a water sprite named Aquamarina, who is not only messing up plumbing all over town, but has also made a home in a fish tank at the pet store, and has turned anyone who sees her into a fish—in the water she is powerful, so the three fairy hunters must come up with a way to trick her onto dry land where she can be overcome.
Identifiers: LCCN 2020002069 | ISBN 9781338627848 (paperback) | ISBN 9781338627855 (library binding) | ISBN 9781338627862 (ebook)
Subjects: LCSH: Fairies—Juvenile fiction. | Water spirits—Juvenile fiction. | Missing persons—Juvenile fiction. | Cousins—Juvenile fiction. | CYAC: Fairies—Fiction. | Water spirits—Fiction. | Missing persons—Fiction. | Cousins—Fiction.
Classification: LCC PZ7.W51937 Pf 2021 | DDC 813.54 [Fic]—dc23
LC record available at https://lccn.loc.gov/2020002069

10 9 8 7 6 5 4 3 2 1   21 22 23 24 25

Printed in China   62
This edition first printing, May 2021
Book design by Sarah Dvojack

Table of Contents

Whenever pixies do escape
Through the old oak tree,
Here is what you have to do
Or trouble there will be.
First find a Pixie Tricker,
The youngest in the land.
Send him to the human world,
The Book of Tricks in hand.
Once he's there, he'll find a girl
Who's only eight years old.
But she's a smart and clever girl
Who's also very bold.
He must ask her for her help,
And if she does agree,
They'll trick the pixies one by one
Till no more do they see.
Only they can do the job.
It's much more than a game.
For if they fail to trick them all,
The world won't be the same!

1

A Bad Day

Violet Briggs was in a bad mood.

Violet hardly ever was in a bad mood. She didn't see the point. She'd rather be happy than be stuck feeling grumpy.

She knew that she should have felt happier today. She was searching for pixies with a real-live fairy named Sprite. But her cousin Leon's complaining was spoiling everything.

"What a waste of time," Leon said. They were in their backyard. "We spent the whole morning looking for pixies. And what did we find? Nothing."

"It wasn't a waste of time," Violet said.

Leon kicked at the grass. "I could have been playing video games," he said.

"Who's stopping you?" Violet asked. "It was your idea to come with us."

"I thought looking for pixies would be exciting," Leon said. "But it's boring. We've been looking for pixies for a week. And we haven't seen any new ones. I bet there aren't any more pixies to find."

Sprite flew in front of Leon's face. Sprite was a small fairy with pale green skin. His wings looked like they were made of rainbows. He had a long spear made from a plant stem tucked into his belt. A tiny bag hung from his waist.

"There are twelve more out there!" Sprite said. "Fourteen fairies escaped from my world. Violet and I caught the first one. And you helped us catch the second one. That leaves twelve."

Violet nodded.

Queen Mab, the fairy queen, had given Sprite *The Book of Tricks*. It told how to trick each pixie in the fairy world. If a pixie escaped, their picture disappeared from the book. You had to trick them to send them back. Then their picture appeared again.

First, Violet and Sprite had tricked a fairy named Pix. Then a gremlin named Jolt had trapped Leon in a video game. She and Sprite had saved Leon. But now Leon knew all about their secret.

"I *know* there are more pixies out there," Violet said. "Hinky Pink made fog and rain. And Sprite and I saw Spoiler last week."

"So where are they now?" Leon asked.

Sprite's wings fluttered. They always did that when he was nervous.

4

"I don't know," Sprite said. "It's strange that we haven't seen one."

Violet held out her finger. Sprite flew over and rested on it.

"Let's eat lunch," Violet told Leon. "Sprite and I will look again in the afternoon. You can stay home if you want."

"Whatever," Leon mumbled.

"Violet! Leon! Get in here right now!" Aunt Anne called from inside their house.

"We'd better go," Violet said. "She sounds mad."

Violet gently put Sprite in her hoodie pocket.

"Watch the wings!" Sprite said.

Violet and Leon walked into the tall yellow house that they shared. Leon and Aunt Anne lived on the first floor. Violet lived on the second floor with her mom and dad.

Aunt Anne and Violet's mom stood in the hallway. Aunt Anne had a big frown on her face. Mrs. Briggs looked worried.

"What have you two been up to?" Aunt Anne asked.

Violet went pale. *Do they know about the fairies?* she thought.

2
A Big Mess

"Follow me," Aunt Anne told Violet and Leon. She walked down the hall and opened the bathroom door. "Look at the big mess you've made."

Puddles of water covered the floor. Water dripped from the faucet.

"I found this faucet gushing with water, and now I can't get it to stop dripping," Aunt Anne said. "I've told you before not to leave it running."

"But, Mom, we didn't!" Leon said.

"It's the same upstairs," said Violet's mom. "Were you playing some kind of game?" She was looking at the bag strapped around Violet's waist. Violet had stuffed it with small tools. A magnifying glass. A tiny flashlight. Sunglasses.

Mom has spotted my fairy-catching bag! Violet thought. She had started bringing it along when they looked for pixies, but her tools had nothing to do with the leaky faucets.

8

Violet thought fast. "No, Mom," she said. "Honest. Maybe the faucets are broken."

"Maybe," her mom said. "But they were fine this morning."

Aunt Anne looked at their faces closely. "I want you two to clean up the mess here and upstairs," she said. "After lunch, we'll all go into town. We'll get some new parts for the faucets."

"But, Mom!" Leon said. "Why should we have to clean it up when we didn't even—"

"Enough, Leon," Aunt Anne said. "Now get to work."

Aunt Anne and Mrs. Briggs went upstairs. Violet got a mop and pail from the hall closet.

Violet started sloshing the mop on the bathroom floor. Sprite flew out of her pocket and sat on the edge of the sink.

Leon found some rags and began to help. "This is going to take forever!"

"You're right!" Violet replied. She sighed. "Now we won't get to look for fairies again until tomorrow."

Suddenly, Sprite pointed to the sink.

"A fairy!" Sprite shouted. "There's a fairy in the sink!"

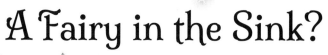

3
A Fairy in the Sink?

"**A** fairy? Really?" Violet asked. She and Leon rushed to the sink.

Water swirled down the drain. There was no fairy in sight.

"Very funny, Sprite," Leon said.

Sprite flew in front of Leon's face.

"I wasn't being funny," he insisted. "I saw a fairy. It was a water sprite."

"Maybe you saw Hinky Pink," Violet said. "He likes to make it rain. Maybe he likes leaky faucets, too."

Sprite shook his head. "It was definitely a water sprite. I saw her!"

"A water sprite?" Leon asked. "What's that?"

"Well, I'm an air sprite," Sprite explained. "I have wings and can fly. A water sprite lives in water. They can breathe underwater, like fish."

"So where is this fish-fairy now?" Leon asked.

"She went down the drain," Sprite said. "I know I saw her!"

Sprite sank back down on the sink. He looked sad.

Violet thought for a minute.

"I believe you," she said. "It makes sense. We know that the escaped pixies like to cause trouble. That water sprite must be *making* our faucets leak."

Sprite's eyes lit up. "Right! Right!" he shouted.

"You mean like how Jolt messed with my video game?" Leon asked.

"Yes," Violet said. "And how Pix made everyone want to play all the time."

Now Leon looked interested. "Let's catch this tricky pixie!"

"First, we need to check *The Book of Tricks*," Violet said. "Let's see if we can find a water sprite with a missing picture. Then we'll know if one has escaped."

"Good idea!" Sprite said as he reached into his bag and took out a tiny book. He flipped through it. "Here's one! I know her. Her name is Aquamarina."

Sprite read the poem aloud from the book.

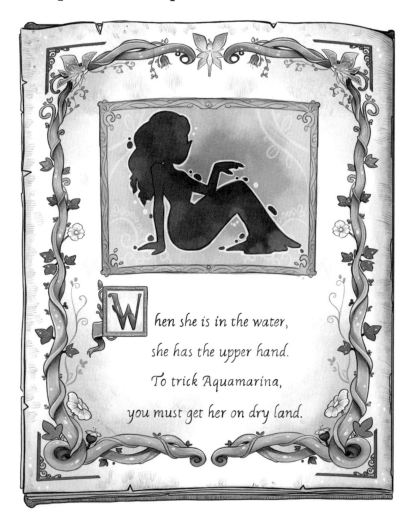

When she is in the water,
she has the upper hand.
To trick Aquamarina,
you must get her on dry land.

"Awesome!" Leon said. "Now we know how to trick her. Let's go."

"We can't," Violet said. "We don't know where to look."

Leon pointed to the drain. "Maybe she went down into the sewer. Sprite can use his magic pixie dust to bring us down there."

Violet wrinkled her nose. "Yuck! I don't want to go down there. Besides, those water pipes go all over town. She could be anywhere by now."

Sprite flew up next to Violet's face. "We need to find her soon," he said. "Aquamarina is one of the trickiest pixies I've ever met!"

A Clue

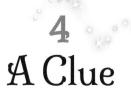

"**W**e need to finish cleaning up," Violet said. "Leon, can you keep mopping? I'll look to see if Aquamarina left any clues behind."

Violet took out her magnifying glass. She looked through it and walked all around the room.

"What are you looking for?" Sprite asked, fluttering next to her.

"I don't know," Violet replied. "I'll know it when I find it."

But Violet didn't find anything that looked like a clue. She and Leon mopped up the water in the bathrooms.

Then Aunt Anne called them to lunch.

Violet and Leon ate their peanut-butter-and-banana sandwiches in silence. They were thinking about where Aquamarina might be. Sprite was tucked into Violet's pocket, and she fed him some tiny pieces of her sandwich.

After lunch, Violet and Leon climbed into the back seat of Aunt Anne's car. Sprite stayed hidden in Violet's pocket.

Mrs. Briggs and Aunt Anne sat up front.

"Off to the hardware store!" Mrs. Briggs said. "Then we can fix the sinks together."

"That sounds like *so* much fun," Leon mumbled, rolling his eyes.

Violet and Leon stared out the windows.

Aunt Anne turned to Violet's mom. "Did you read the news today?" she asked.

"I did," Mrs. Briggs answered. She turned on the car radio. Violet knew she did that when she didn't want Violet to hear what she was talking about.

Violet leaned forward and tried to hear.

"It's terrible," Aunt Anne said. "Five people have disappeared in the last few days. And here's something weird: Each one of them was near a lake, a pool, or a pond when they vanished!"

"That sounds serious," Violet whispered to Sprite and Leon. "And very strange. Sprite, I think this might be a clue!"

5
A Cry for Help

"Did you say something, Violet?" her mom asked from the front seat.

"Uh, no," Violet replied.

Aunt Anne pulled the car into a parking lot.

They all walked out to the sidewalk. A long line of people waited outside Caldwell's Hardware.

At the end of the line, Violet spotted her friend Brittany Brightman. Brittany looked nice, as always. She wore an orange headband in her dark braided hair. A necklace with a tiny letter *B* dangling from it hung around her neck.

They got in line behind Brittany and her dad.

"What's going on?" Aunt Anne asked Mr. Brightman.

"I have a leaky faucet," he replied. "It seems like everybody in town does. Kind of weird, isn't it?"

Leon nudged Violet. She knew he was thinking the same thing. The water sprite was very busy!

"There's nothing to do but wait," Violet's mom said cheerfully.

"Great," Leon muttered. "We'll be here all day."

Violet sighed. She knew he was right.

Brittany tapped her dad's arm. "Can Violet, Leon, and I go to the pet store instead of waiting in line?" she asked.

Violet liked to visit Miller's Pet Shop. It had lots of colorful fish, beautiful birds, and lizards that looked like tiny dinosaurs.

Violet looked at her mom. "Please? It's right next door."

Violet's mom turned to Aunt Anne. "It *is* next door," she said. "And I know the owner, Joe Miller. They'll be all right in there."

Aunt Anne nodded. "Fine with me."

"Thanks!" Violet cried. She and Leon followed Brittany into the store.

The store was empty, except for Mr. Miller. He was filling the birds' water dishes. Violet noticed that *his* faucet was leaking, too.

"Hi, Mr. Miller," Violet said. "Our parents said we could look around while they wait in line at the hardware store."

Mr. Miller didn't smile at Violet like he usually did. He just stared straight ahead.

"That's nice," he said in a flat voice.

"Mr. Miller?" Violet asked. "Are you okay?"

He didn't answer. It wasn't like Mr. Miller at all. He was always very friendly. That's when Violet noticed something else weird. His eyes were sparkling with blue light.

Violet was worried. She needed to talk to Sprite, but she couldn't do that in front of Brittany.

Brittany didn't know about Sprite. Violet wasn't sure what her friend would do or think. Brittany was in charge of the second-grade newspaper. She'd probably put Sprite on the front page! And that would be very bad.

"Ooh, look at the pretty fish," Brittany said, spotting a fish tank by the door. "Violet, let's look over here."

"I'll be right there," Violet said. "I want to see the lizards first."

Violet grabbed Leon by the sleeve. She dragged him over to the lizard tank.

"What are you doing?" Leon asked.

Violet took Sprite out of her pocket. "Mr. Miller is acting super weird, and it looked like his eyes were sparkling," Violet told them. "Sprite, do you know what's wrong with him?"

Sprite nodded. "It looks like he's under a fairy spell," he said. "I've seen this before."

"Leaky faucets," said Violet. "Five missing people. And now Mr. Miller's under a spell."

"I think that Aquamarina might be behind all this," Sprite said.

"Eeeeeeeeeeeeeeeeeek!"
Violet, Sprite, and Leon spun around.
The scream came from Brittany!

6
Aquamarina

Violet and Leon ran to Brittany. Sprite flew behind Violet. Then he landed on her shoulder and peeked out from behind her ponytail.

Brittany was pointing to the fish tank. Her eyes were wide.

"Brittany, are you okay?" Violet asked.

But Brittany didn't answer. She just kept pointing.

Violet looked inside the fish tank. Five colorful fish swam there.

Those fish look a little strange, Violet thought. *They all have very big eyes with long eyelashes. Their noses and mouths look almost human. And one of the fish is wearing glasses! Did Aquamarina create these strange fish somehow?*

Violet gasped. But she didn't want to alarm Brittany.

"These fish do look a little weird," Violet said. "Is that why you screamed?"

Brittany shook her head.

"There," she whispered. "Back there."

Violet looked inside the tank again, and Brittany pointed to a small toy castle.

A tiny woman swam behind the castle. She was the same size as Sprite, but with blue-green skin. She wore a dress made out of fish scales. Her long hair looked like seaweed. She almost looked like a mermaid, but she didn't have a fishtail. Instead, she had legs and webbed feet. Her hands were webbed, too.

The castle was a toy, but the woman wasn't. She was real.

"That's Aquamarina," Sprite whispered to Violet. "We found her!"

Violet didn't know what to do next. They could not catch Aquamarina with Brittany right there.

But Leon forgot about keeping the pixies a secret. "Hey!" he shouted. "It's the fish-fairy! Let's get her!"

"Oh dear," Sprite said. "This won't be good."

Aquamarina turned to face them. Her eyes flashed with blue-green light.

"*Eeeeeeeeeeeeeeeeeeek!*" Brittany screamed again.

Aquamarina stared at Brittany from inside the fish tank. The light in her eyes got brighter and brighter.

"Brittany, get away from the tank!" Violet yelled, reaching for her friend's hand. But she wasn't fast enough.

Two beams of blue-green light shot out of the tank. They zapped Brittany.

Brittany's body glowed brightly. Then she disappeared before their eyes!

"Brittany!" Violet cried. She looked in the tank.

Instead of five fish, there were now six.

The new fish had glasses just like Brittany's. A necklace with the letter *B* hung around her body.

"Oh no!" Sprite cried. "Aquamarina has turned Brittany into a fish!"

7
Leon's Mistake

"**B**rittany is a f-f-fish," Leon stammered. He stepped back from the tank.

Aquamarina turned and looked at Leon. Her eyes started to glow again.

Sprite flew in front of Leon. "Aquamarina! Stop that right now!"

Aquamarina paused. Then she smiled.

"Why, hello, Sprite. Fancy seeing you here," she said. Bubbles came out of her mouth as she talked. Her voice sounded fuzzy to Violet.

I'm a little scared of her, Violet thought. *But I've got to help Brittany!*

"What did you do to our friend?" Violet asked. "Please change her back!"

Aquamarina laughed. More tiny bubbles filled the water.

"Why would I do that? She's better this way," the water sprite said. "Fish are so much nicer than humans. They don't yell or scream."

Violet gasped. *The other fish in the tank must be the missing people from the news! Aquamarina used her magic on them.*

"You're so mean!" Violet cried.

"Don't worry, your human friends will live happy lives in this tank," Aquamarina promised her.

Sprite flew up to the tank. He took a gold medal out of his bag.

"I am a Royal Pixie Tricker now," Sprite told Aquamarina. "By order of the fairy queen, I command you to change back Brittany and the other five humans you have in there with you! Then you must return to the Otherworld."

Aquamarina did a graceful somersault in the water. She smiled again.

"No, thank you," she replied. "I'll never leave the human world!"

Sprite sat on the top of the fish tank. "Why not?" he asked Aquamarina.

"Queen Mab can't tell me what to do in this world," replied the water sprite. "And here, there is water everywhere! I had fun causing all those faucets to leak. I love the way they drip, drip, drip."

"I knew it!" Violet said.

"I was having so much fun in this town that I decided to stay," Aquamarina said. "Mr. Miller's fish tanks are the perfect home. I put him under a little spell so that he doesn't mind that I'm here."

"You're living out in the open in the human world," said Sprite. "Isn't that a little risky?"

"Just a little bit," Aquamarina said. "Five humans saw me. That's why I turned them into fish. Aren't they beautiful?"

Violet glared at her. "That wasn't a very nice thing to do."

"That's your opinion," Aquamarina replied. "And don't even *try* to trick me. I'm too smart for that."

"You're a bad fairy!" Leon cried, and he leaned into the tank.

Sprite flew between Leon and the tank. Leon stopped.

"You're right, Aquamarina," Sprite said. "We won't be able to trick you."

"Of course not," she replied calmly. She began to comb her long hair with a small seashell. "I think you should all go home. Or I just might change my mind and turn you into guppies!"

Sprite waved his hand at Violet and Leon. They followed him back to the lizard tank.

"Sprite, why did you stop me?" Leon asked.

"Because we need to think of a good way to trick her," Sprite said.

"Sprite is right," Violet said. "We have to think of a plan first. A way to get her on dry land like *The Book of Tricks* said."

"That's easy," Leon said. "We just reach into the tank and scoop her out."

Violet shook her head. "No, that's too dangerous. She'll turn us into fish!"

"Well, if we don't do something fast, she'll turn everyone in town into fish!" Leon argued.

He ran across the room and plunged his hand into the fish tank. Aquamarina swam back and forth. She was too fast. Leon couldn't catch her.

Then Violet saw a light glowing in the tank.

A blue-green light.

"Watch out, Leon!" Violet yelled. "Aquamarina's going to zap you!"

8
The Fish Boy

Violet ran to Leon as fast as she could. Sprite whizzed past her.

The blue-green light got brighter. Two beams of light zoomed toward Leon . . .

Sprite reached into his bag and pulled out some glittering dust.

"To the parking lot!" Sprite yelled. He threw the dust over himself, Leon, and Violet.

Achoo! Pixie dust always made Violet sneeze.

Her body tingled. Bright white lights shone around them all. She closed her eyes.

When she opened them, she was standing in the parking lot behind the pet store.

Sprite flew in front of Violet.

"Good job, Sprite," Violet said. "Just in time. You saved—Leon?"

Violet tried not to scream. Leon stood next to her. But he wasn't the same old Leon.

Leon's eyes were big and bulging, like fish eyes. He had shiny scales on his face. His ears looked like fins.

Aquamarina must have started to cast her spell, Violet guessed. *But then Sprite stopped the spell in the middle. So now Leon is part fish. A fish boy!*

"Oh dear," Sprite said. "Oh dear, oh dear."

"Oh dear, what?" Leon asked.

"Uh, nothing," Violet said quickly.

Then she whispered to Sprite, "Don't say anything. I don't want Leon to freak out."

"Right," Sprite whispered back. "Besides, as soon as we trick Aquamarina, Leon will change back."

"I'm so thirsty," Leon said. "Is there any water around here?"

"Later," Violet told him. "Now we have to make a plan. We have to figure out how to get Aquamarina onto dry land."

"I'm hungry," Leon said. "Does anyone have any worms? Or maybe some fish food? Mmmm, fish food." He licked his lips.

Leon did not seem to care about their pixie-tricking mission anymore.

Violet sank down on the curb.

"How can we get Aquamarina out of the tank?" she asked Sprite. "If we go near her, she'll turn us into fish. And *then* we won't be able to help *anyone*."

"That's true," Sprite said.

Violet brightened. "Can we say her name backward three times? That's worked before."

Sprite frowned. "That only works on small magic spells," he said. "Turning people into fish is a big magic spell."

Violet had another idea. "What if I wear my hoodie backward? That helped me escape from a fairy ring once."

Sprite shook his head. "Nope. We have to trick Aquamarina out of her tank and onto dry land. That's the only way we'll break her spells and send her back."

"I've got it!" Leon cried.

"You do?" Violet asked.

Leon pulled something out of his pocket. "Rats. It's just gum. I thought it was fish food," he said.

Violet sighed. *Leon is a fish boy. Brittany and five other people are fish,* she thought. *We can't go back in the pet store because Aquamarina will zap us. So how can we get her on dry land?*

Violet didn't know what to do, and she knew that her mom and Aunt Anne would be looking for them any minute.

"That's it, Sprite," Violet said, frowning. "I give up!"

9
The Fairy Queen

"We can't give up," Sprite said.

"I don't know what else to do," Violet answered.

Suddenly, Sprite's magic bag began to glow. A soft purple light shone through the bag.

"What's happening?" Violet asked.

"I'm not sure," Sprite said. "This has never happened before."

Sprite slowly and carefully reached into the bag. Violet held her breath as Sprite pulled out a glowing purple stone.

The light on the stone faded. Then a picture began to appear. Violet leaned in to see it.

It was a woman's face. She had long, wavy pink hair and brown skin. Her eyes were purple, like Violet's. She wore a shimmering crown on her head.

The woman smiled.

Sprite bowed. "Queen Mab," Sprite said. "I am at your service."

Violet gasped. It was the fairy queen! The queen who sent Sprite to this world.

Violet had never met a queen before. She bowed, also. "I am at your service, too."

Leon pushed his way in front of Violet. "I'm thirsty," he complained.

"Leon!" Violet said. "It's the fairy queen!"

"Does she have any fish food?" Leon asked.

Sprite bowed before the queen again. "Your Majesty, I'm sorry about the boy. He's under a spell."

Queen Mab laughed. Violet thought it sounded like tinkling bells.

"I understand," the queen said. "It is not his fault."

"Thank you," Sprite said.

"I must speak with you, Sprite," said the queen. "And you, Violet. You two must not give up!"

"I'm sorry, Your Majesty," Violet said. "But I can't think of a way to stop Aquamarina."

"And I can't come up with a plan, either," Sprite said. "You must be very angry with me." He hung his head.

The queen shook her head. "Of course not. I am very proud of you," she said. "You and Violet have already tricked two fairies—Pix and Jolt."

"But we still have twelve more fairies to go," Sprite said.

"You will do it," said the queen. "But there are strong forces against you. Finn knows you are here."

Sprite's pale green skin turned even paler. "Finn? Is he in the human world?"

58

The queen nodded.

"Who's Finn?" Violet asked.

"Finn is a powerful fairy. A great wizard," Sprite answered.

"It was he who led the other thirteen fairies in the escape," added the queen. "He is in your world. When he found out you sent Pix and Jolt back to the Otherworld, he was not happy. He has been helping the other fairies hide from you."

"So we were lucky to find Aquamarina," Violet said.

"Yes," replied Queen Mab.

"It doesn't matter that we know where she is," Sprite said. "We'll never be able to trick her."

"Don't worry, my Royal Pixie Tricker," said the queen. "You will find the answer *in time*."

"But what *is* the answer?" Sprite asked.

Queen Mab smiled. Then her face slowly faded, and the stone went dark.

10
The Queen's Clue

Sprite looked down at the purple stone. "This is terrible. Queen Mab's gone, and I still don't know what to do!"

Violet jumped to her feet. "The queen said we can do it, Sprite. I believe her."

Sprite nodded. "You're right. If Queen Mab says we can do it, then we'll do it."

Violet thought for a minute. "It shouldn't be so hard to get Aquamarina on dry land," she said. "It's just that she might turn us into fish."

"She'll never turn *me* into a fish!" Leon boasted, and Violet and Sprite didn't correct him.

"Is there some way that we can protect ourselves from the spell?" Violet asked.

Sprite shook his head. "It's a strong spell."

Violet thought some more. "The queen said we'd find the answer *in time*. Maybe she meant exactly what she said. Is there some way we could use time to help us?"

Sprite frowned. Then his eyes lit up. "Of course!" he said. "A time spell! I should have thought of it before!"

"What is it?" asked Violet.

"A time spell has the power to protect you from another spell for a little bit of time," Sprite said. "Usually five minutes."

"That's plenty of time," Violet said.

Sprite blushed. "I am not very good at casting time spells. Mine only last about one minute."

"Maybe that's all the time we will need," Violet said. "I think I have a plan!"

11
Time for a Spell

Violet peeked around the wall of the pet store. Her mom and Aunt Anne were almost inside the hardware store next door.

"Let's hurry," Violet said. She grabbed Leon.

"Can I have fish food now?" Leon asked.

Sprite sprinkled pixie dust over them. "To the lizard tank!"

In a flash, they were back inside Miller's Pet Shop. They huddled behind the lizard tank. Aquamarina was swimming peacefully in the fish tank with Brittany and the other fish.

"Cast your time spell now," Violet told Sprite.

"I'm on it!" Sprite said.

Violet turned to Leon. "Leon, count out sixty seconds so we'll know when time's up."

"I'm thirsty," Leon said.

"Just start counting, please," Violet said.

Sprite closed his eyes. He sprinkled more pixie dust over them.

Violet didn't feel much different. But there was a little buzzing sound in her head.

"My time spell is working," Sprite said. "Now hurry!"

"Okay," said Violet.

"One fish food, two fish food, three fish food . . ." Leon counted.

Violet ran up to the counter.

"Mr. Miller, may I please borrow a wrench?" Violet asked.

The dazed store owner reached under the counter. He handed the tool to Violet.

"Have a nice day," he said.

"Thank you," Violet replied. She rushed behind the counter to the sink with the leaky faucet.

"Ten fish food, eleven fish food . . ." Leon counted.

Violet began to fix the leaky faucet. She wasn't sure how to do it exactly. But for her plan to work, all she had to do was try.

Aquamarina saw Violet at the sink. She stopped swimming.

Violet pretended to ignore her and kept turning the wrench. She watched Aquamarina from the corner of her eye.

Aquamarina swam up to the top of the water. She stuck out her head. "What are you doing?"

"I'm fixing the faucet," Violet said. "It's leaking."

"I know it's leaking!" said the water sprite. "I did that myself. I love the drip, drip, drip it makes."

Violet tried not to smile. This was just what she had planned. Aquamarina would try to stop her. And in order to do that, she'd *have* to come on dry land.

"Twenty-eight fish food, twenty-nine fish food . . ." Leon counted.

"Well, I don't like the drip, drip, drip," Violet said. "I'm going to make it stop."

"Don't you dare!" Aquamarina cried. She climbed onto the edge of the fish tank. Her eyes began to glow. She aimed two beams of blue-green light at Violet. Violet dropped the wrench and closed her eyes.

Uh-oh, she thought. *If Sprite's time spell doesn't work, I'll be turned into a fish!*

12
Fish Food!

Violet's skin tingled. Then Aquamarina's beams fizzled out.

Violet slowly opened her eyes. She was still human.

Sprite's time spell had worked!

Aquamarina scowled. "That spell should have worked!" she cried. "If magic won't stop you, I will stop you myself!"

Aquamarina started to climb out of the fish tank. Then she stopped. She slid back into the tank and gripped the rim.

"I know what you are trying to do!" Aquamarina said. She pointed a tiny finger at Violet. "You're trying to trick me."

Sprite flew up next to Aquamarina. "No, we're not," he said, and he crossed his fingers behind his back. "Go stop Violet from fixing the faucet. Don't you want to hear the drip, drip, drip?"

Aquamarina dove back into the water.

"It's not going to work," she told Sprite. "I'm too clever to be tricked. And I'm much too happy here in the human world to risk having to leave."

Then she glared at Sprite.

"Well, I *was* happy," she said. "Until you came and tried to spoil everything."

Aquamarina's eyes glowed blue-green. She shot two beams of light at Sprite.

Nothing happened.

"You must be using magic to dodge my spells," Aquamarina said. "A protection spell, maybe?"

Leon ran up to the fish tank.

"Fifty-nine fish food, sixty fish food!" he cried. "Time's up. Now Sprite's spell won't work anymore!"

Violet cringed. "Leon!"

Aquamarina grinned. "So you *were* using a time spell! But it's over now. Perfect! I've got you all where I want you."

"Leon, Sprite, let's get out of here!" Violet cried.

Aquamarina's
eyes began
to glow again.

But Leon didn't
run. He sniffed the
air. "Fish food?" he
asked.

Flakes of fish food floated on top of the water.
"Fish food!" Leon yelled.

He tried to jump into the fish tank. But he
knocked it over instead. The tank fell to the
floor with a crash.

Smash! The glass shattered into a million
pieces, and water gushed everywhere.

Brittany and the other fish flopped around
on the floor.

The crash sent the water sprite soaring through the air. The glow in her eyes faded. She sailed through the open door.

Aquamarina landed outside the door and skidded across the sidewalk.

"Oh no," she said. "Dry land!"

A whirling tunnel of wind appeared out of nowhere. The wind scooped up Aquamarina.

"Fish are much better than humans!" she yelled.

The three Pixie Trickers watched as the water sprite disappeared into the tunnel.

13
A Fishy Tale

"**W**e did it!" Violet cheered. "We tricked Aquamarina!"

Sprite flew up and hid behind Violet's ponytail. "Look," he whispered. "Aquamarina's spells are broken."

Violet turned. The six flopping fish were gone. In their place were six soggy people: the five missing adults, and—

"Brittany!" Violet cried. She helped her friend up off the floor. "Are you all right?"

Brittany looked confused. "I think so," she said, trying to wring out her dress. "What happened? How did I get all wet? And why is there broken glass everywhere?"

"You mean you don't remember?" Violet asked.

Brittany shook her head. "I was looking at the fish. Then I was on the floor."

Violet thought fast. "Leon knocked over the fish tank by mistake," she said.

That reminded her.

"Leon?" Violet found her cousin on the floor. There were fish food flakes all over his face. But his scales and fishy ears were gone. And his eyes weren't bulging.

Violet had to make sure he was back to normal. "Leon, do you want some fish food?"

"What are you talking about?" Leon asked. "What happened to the fish-fairy?"

"I'll explain later," Violet said.

Just then, Mr. Brightman, Aunt Anne, and Violet's mom stepped into the pet store. Sprite quickly hid in Violet's hoodie pocket.

"What's going on here?" Mrs. Briggs asked. Her eyes were wide.

Aunt Anne stared at Leon. "You're soaking wet!" she cried.

"You, too, Brittany," Mr. Brightman said.

"I . . . Violet says that Leon knocked over the fish tank," Brittany said.

"It was an accident," Violet explained.

Mr. Miller seemed like he was back to normal, too. But he looked just as confused as everyone else. "I'm not exactly sure what happened," he said. "But there's no harm done. That was an empty tank."

"Let's get you home and dry you off, Leon," Aunt Anne said.

"You too, Brittany," Mr. Brightman said, shaking his head. He looked at Aunt Anne. "Kids are full of surprises!"

On the ride home, Aunt Anne turned up the radio. Violet knew they were talking about the mess in the pet store.

Violet opened her hoodie pocket a tiny bit.

"Let's check the book," she whispered to Sprite.

Sprite gave Violet *The Book of Tricks*. She found the page about Aquamarina. There used to be a blank square above the poem. But now there was a picture of Aquamarina on the page.

When she is in the water,
she has the upper hand.
To trick Aquamarina,
you must get her on dry land.

"We really did it," Violet whispered.

"You mean *I* did it," Leon said. "I'm the one who knocked over the fish tank."

"Good job," Sprite whispered back.

But Sprite was frowning. Violet thought he looked worried.

"What's wrong?" she asked.

"I'm thinking about something the queen said," Sprite replied.

Violet remembered the queen's face in the purple stone. She still couldn't believe she had seen Queen Mab.

"The queen said something about a strong fairy—a wizard," Violet said.

"Finn," Sprite said. He shivered. "He is very bad. And now that Finn knows I'm here, we're in big trouble!"

Leon's eyes grew wide. "What will he do to us?"

"He will try to stop us from tricking the pixies," Sprite replied. "And we need to find eleven more fairies, including Finn."

Violet frowned. "If he is helping them, it will be harder than ever to trick them!"

About the Creators

Tracey West has written several book series for children, including the *New York Times* bestselling Dragon Masters series. She is thrilled that her first series, Pixie Tricks, is being introduced to a new generation of readers.

Xavier Bonet lives in Barcelona, in a little village near the Mediterranean Sea called Sant Boi. He loves illustrating, magic, and all retro stuff. But above all, he loves spending time with his two children—they are his real inspiration.

Pixie Tricks
The Pet Store Sprite
Questions and Activities

At first, Violet thinks that Hinky Pink might be to blame for the leaky faucets. Why does she think this? Turn back to page 4.

In the car, Mrs. Briggs turns on the radio when she talks to Aunt Anne. Why does she do this? Reread page 19.

Mr. Miller is behaving strangely when Violet first sees him in the pet store. How does Violet know something is wrong?

Queen Mab tells Sprite and Violet that Finn has escaped from the Otherworld. Who is Finn? What is he doing to cause trouble? Reread page 59.

Aquamarina turns Brittany into a fish. What would you look like if you were turned into a fish? Draw a picture of yourself in the tank!